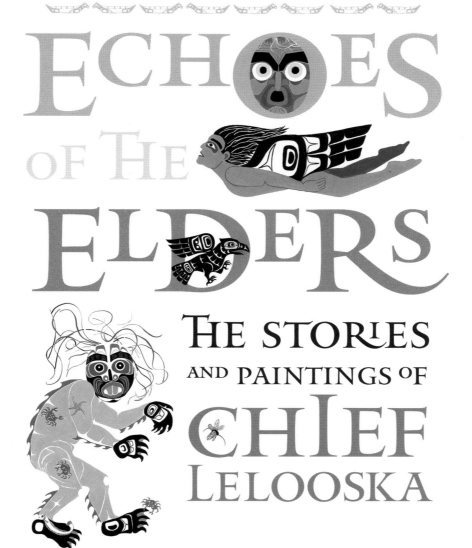

ECHOES OF THE ELDERS

THE STORIES AND PAINTINGS OF CHIEF LELOOSKA

EDITED BY CHRISTINE NORMANDIN

A DK INK BOOK
DK PUBLISHING, INC.

IN ASSOCIATION WITH

CALLAWAY EDITIONS

THIS BOOK IS DEDICATED TO THE LATE JAMES OL (AUL) SEWIDE III
AND THE HOUSE OF SEWIDE.

The idea for this book of Northwest Coast Indian folktales surfaced about five years ago, when Chief Lelooska first found out he was gravely ill. He told me that, for the first time in his life, he was forced to face the fact of his own mortality. He recalled vividly something one of the elders had told him many years before when he was doing research on the old stories: "Don't take these stories to the grave with you." The elder then entrusted into Lelooska's care stories of the Kwakiutl so that they could be passed on to new generations.

During his recovery, Chief Lelooska began the process of recording stories and painting illustrations. A little over three years ago he enlisted my help in editing the stories he had selected as material for a book. From the beginning, Chief Lelooska's high regard for teachers and his love of children have guided the focus of this book. He wanted it to be primarily for them.

In early 1996, Chief Lelooska was diagnosed with terminal cancer. At that point the book of folktales became a priority. He felt that he had to keep his promise to the elders who had shared their memories with him and without whom he would never have been able to pursue his lifelong passion for storytelling.

In his last few weeks, Chief Lelooska continued to paint illustrations for the book, now called *Echoes of the Elders,* recorded audio versions of the stories, and reviewed rough layouts that were sent from the publisher. He was pleased with the book and excited about its completion.

On September 5, 1996, Chief Lelooska died. He is gone, but his work lives on in *Echoes of the Elders* — his promise fulfilled.

CHRISTINE NORMANDIN

THIS COLLECTION OF FOLKTALES IS ABOUT A TIME LONG AGO WHEN THERE WERE NO NATURAL LAWS AS WE KNOW THEM TODAY. THERE WERE NO STARS IN THE HEAVENS, AND THERE WAS NO SUN OR MOON IN THE SKY. THERE WAS NO DAYLIGHT. SPIRITS AND ANIMALS DWELLED IN THIS DARK WORLD FULL OF MAGIC. MANY OF THEM COULD CHANGE THEIR SHAPES AND TRANSFORM THEMSELVES INTO HUMANS OR OTHER MYSTERIOUS CREATURES. EVENTUALLY SOME OF THE ANIMALS STAYED IN HUMAN FORM AND BECAME THE ANCESTORS OF THE NORTHWEST COAST PEOPLES OF TODAY.

The humans did not rule the animals. They attempted to live in harmony with nature and the other tribes of beings that roamed the earth. All living and nonliving things had spirits that had to be respected, and there was a common language understood by all.

Some animals and humans had special powers, which they called their *dlugwee,* or supernatural treasure. This power could be acquired by one who was worthy. It could also be taken away. The most powerful of all was Raven. He could do anything he wanted to do. He created the first humans and brought the sun, stars, moon, and fresh water to the world. While he did much good, Raven also was known as a trickster, glutton, liar, and thief.

The italicized words in these stories are phonetic spellings of the Kwakwala language spoken by the Kwakwaka Wakw (Kwakiutl) people.

CHRISTINE NORMANDIN

🐦 INTRODUCTION

THOUSANDS OF TALES ONCE SERVED AS THE LITERATURE OF THE INDIANS OF THE NORTH-WEST COAST OF NORTH AMERICA. THE PASSAGE OF TIME, CHANGES IN CULTURE, DESTRUCTION OF VILLAGES, AND "CIVILIZATION" PROGRAMS HAVE TAKEN A TERRIBLE TOLL ON THESE TRADITIONS. SCHOLARS ESTIMATE THAT AS FEW AS TEN PERCENT OF THE AGE-OLD TALES, HISTORIES, AND LEGENDS SURVIVE TODAY. SOME OF THESE ACCOUNTS ARE PRESERVED ONLY IN FRAGMENTS, AND MANY LACK THE STORY ELEMENTS THAT GAVE THEM FORM AND POWER.

This volume represents a small part of the literary legacy of the vast forested shoreline of the Northwest Coast of North America. The stories come from a land where the sea dominates. Its fog, mist, rain, and warm currents give shape to the region's climate and abundant food resources. Its shoreline is heavily covered with the world's largest temperate rain forest. Towering sentinels of spruce, hemlock, cedar, and fir rise to the heavens, blocking out the light and casting deep shadows across the needle-covered floor. The rivers are lined with alder, willow, and dense brush.

In this dark, sometimes somber land lived many tribes. They included the Kwakiutl, Haida, Tlingit, Tsimshian, Bella Coola, and the Nootka. They were wealthy people. Their easy access to bountiful runs of salmon and other foods gave them the leisure to develop a rich culture. They constructed huge houses, developed elaborate ceremonies, carved masks and totems, accompanied their dances with drums and whistles, and told the younger generations why the world was the way it was.

Culture is a human heritage passed from generation to generation. It is the tie that binds families, villages, tribes, and nations. Culture is something learned; it is a legacy of sharing. The oral tradition—the oldest form of human transfer of culture—educates, entertains, and expresses the literary artistry of the storyteller. Storytelling is a complex undertaking. It requires an excellent memory and attention to the story details and characters. The accomplished storyteller inflects and modulates the voice, uses gestures, looks directly at the audience, glances away, and varies the cadence of delivery.

The tales in this book were once recounted by Lelooska, who was a master storyteller, carver, painter, and teacher of the culture and history of the Indians of the Northwest Coast. The grandson of a Cherokee who impressed on his descendants the importance of their Indian heritage, Lelooska was given his name by the Nez Perce when he was twelve. His name means "he who cuts against wood with a knife," a prophetic designation for a man who became renowned for his carvings. Today, his carvings and paintings grace public buildings, corporate offices, and the homes of collectors. Lelooska lived with his family of four generations of artists in Ariel, Washington, in the shadow of Mount St. Helens. For nearly forty years he and his family shared their knowledge with thousands of students and other learners. Their evening performances in a cedar-plank house with a central firepit enthralled visitors. His storytelling was that of a master at the craft of oral literature.

In recognition of his skills and dedication to Indian ways, the late James Sewide, a hereditary chief of the Southern Kwakiutl tribe, adopted Lelooska and his family in 1968 by formal potlatch ceremony. Sewide gave Lelooska and his family the right to use the stories, masks, and dances of his family. Today many of the traditional dances of the Kwakiutl are performed with articulated face masks, the artwork that was carved by Lelooska. The connections between Lelooska and the Northwest Coast Indians were founded upon years of conversations with elders, study, travel, and exploration of the traditional Indian cultures of the region.

The stories in this book speak of a time when the world was different than today. They tell of the creatures of Mother Earth who behaved very much like humans, even when there were no humans in the world. The stories provide important lessons to listeners of all ages. Those who heard these stories in ages past, an experience that occurred during the months of the long moons of the dark, wet winters, received a remarkable education. The stories were the primary means of passing on the tribal memory. They recounted how the world had come to be, why things were named as they were, and how humans should act. They speak through time to listeners and readers today.

The tales in this collection, here in print for the first time, perpetuate the tradition of Indian storytelling. They retain the traditional storylines, repeat the important rituals and magical number "four" of the Kwakiutl, and fill in the setting, perhaps less familiar to those who have not visited coastal British Columbia or southeast Alaska. The stories also confirm the privilege of the teller to recount the tale in a way that makes it a special version, recognizable but a little different than the way another might tell it. These tales are a part of the land and a mirror to the people who are the tribes of the Northwest Coast of North America.

STEPHEN DOW BECKHAM
Pamplin Professor of History, Lewis & Clark College, Portland, Oregon
1996

CANADA

TLINGIT

TSIMSHIAN

British Columbia

HAIDA

BELLA COOLA

KWAKIUTL

NOOTKA

SALISH

UNITED STATES

Seattle
Washington

Oregon
Portland

Pacific Ocean

North America

Pacific Ocean

PEOPLE OF THE

NORTHWEST COAST

THE OLD OWL WITCH

ONCE THERE WAS A BEAUTIFUL VILLAGE. TREES TOWERED INTO THE SKY BEHIND IT. A BROAD OPEN BEACH STRETCHED BEFORE IT, AND AT ONE END THERE WAS A PILE OF HUGE ROCKS THAT THE PEOPLE CALLED ROCKY POINT.

The people had good fishing and hunting grounds. They were rich and happy. The village was a lively place with many laughing children. Then something terrible happened.

The children often played among the houses and in the nearby forest, for it was quite safe there. But the parents told the children they must never go deep into the forest. And especially they must never, ever go into that part of the forest where the old hut stood.

"A very strange creature lives there," the parents warned. "That creature, or whatever it is, has been there for a long time. It has never bothered us, so we must never bother it."

The children obeyed their parents, but after awhile some of the bolder ones decided to find the hut and watch for the strange creature. The hut was built of old discarded boards and poles, tree branches, moss, and sticks. It looked more like a beaver's den than the house of something human!

During the daylight the children watched and watched, but no one ever came out. Only late in the evening, just as the parents were calling them into the house, could the

children hear a faint stirring inside the hut.

This excited the imaginations of the children. They wanted to find out what lived in that strange little dwelling, so each day they crept closer and closer to the hut.

"Come out! Come out!" called the children. "We want to see what you look like!" Some of the children even threw rocks and sticks at the hut. But still no creature appeared. The persistent children continued to do this day after day.

Finally one evening, just at nightfall when all the people were gathered around their cooking fires enjoying their meals and telling stories, a strange figure appeared. It hovered in the doorway of the great cedar house, in the shadows where the firelight could not reveal its appearance. The people only saw that the figure was low and squat. Its hollow voice sounded like someone speaking from a deep hole in the ground.

"I have never bothered you," said the figure. "I wish only to be left alone. Leave me in peace and no harm will come to you or your mischievous children. I warn you, leave me in peace or something terrible will happen!"

Then the shadowy figure disappeared into the darkness. The people could hear owls calling to each other in the forest, but strangely there seemed to be a great many more owls than usual.

For a time the children obeyed their parents, but soon they grew bored with their usual games. They decided they would again try to solve the mystery of what lived in the ramshackle hut. They sneaked to the hut and began throwing rocks and howling and yelling insults, and thoroughly misbehaving themselves.

As dark surrounded the village the mysterious figure again appeared in the shadows. "I have warned you once!" hissed the creature. "Your children continue to annoy me, even though I do you and them no harm. Do not, I say, do not let

this happen again!" Then the creature faded into the night. Many more owls called out in the darkness.

The frightened children stayed in the village and were well behaved for a long time after that. But they could not forget the excitement of sneaking into the forest. And they longed to see what the strange creature in the hut looked like. So the children went to the hut again and threw rocks and yelled insults. A third time the mysterious creature visited the village to demand that it be allowed to live in peace.

Again the children obeyed. But finally their curiosity overcame their fear, and they went to the hut a fourth time.

They threw sticks and rocks and even dared to pull branches from the dwelling itself.

That night the figure appeared in the village once again. The people could feel its anger like the searing heat from a fire.

"Four times I have come to you pleading for peace," it cried. "Four is a magic number. I will come no more. Something dreadful will happen if you do not control your children. You will suffer the consequences! I wish only to be left alone!"

The figure stepped forward, and the flickering firelight revealed its huge, staring yellow eyes and long wild hair. It carried a wooden staff. The top of the staff was carved in the shape of an owl, which moved and turned its head.

In the forest great numbers of owls hooted. The strange creature stared at the people. Its fierce eyes seemed to pierce each one of them. Then it was gone!

The village parents were concerned. They did not know if this creature was a spirit or a ghost or some dreadful being that humans were not meant to see or understand. They scolded the children and told them they would be severely punished if they ever went near the hut again.

For a long time the children obeyed, but then they forgot the creature's four warnings. A few bold and disobedient children led the others deep into the forest and deep into trouble again. The foolish children began to throw sticks and rocks at the hut and call out insults. The sun sank slowly into the sea, and it grew darker and darker.

Suddenly the rotten hide covering the door of the hut flew open. Out stepped the mysterious creature wrapped in a robe of featherlike material. Its hands were claws, and it grasped the same wooden staff with the carved owl that blinked its eyes and clicked its beak. The creature's feet were more like bird feet than human feet. Between its yellow eyes was a sharp hooked nose.

"You would not listen!" bellowed the creature. "Now you will learn more than you ever wanted to know about me. I am the Owl Witch, the Chief of all the Owl People. My power is great! If you had left me alone there would be no problem. But now your parents must learn that children must obey!"

The Owl Witch lifted her staff, and all the owls in the forest began to hoot. They circled over the children with their gray wings spread wide. One owl lit on the old Owl Witch's head and glared fiercely at the children.

Back in the village the parents were worried. Night was falling and the children were not home. The forest echoed with the calls of many owls.

Deep in the forest the Owl Witch waved her staff over the children and began to sing a strange, haunting song. As she sang the children grew smaller and smaller, except for their ears which remained rather large. Then the children grew long slender tails, and in a few moments the Owl Witch had transformed all the children into furry, little mice!

The frightened mice scattered into the forest to hide. The owls pursued them, and a great noise arose from the hooting and squeaking and squealing. Then a terrible silence fell upon the forest!

After that there was no joy in the village at rocky point, for all the children were gone. The people went to live among other tribes, and their houses slowly decayed.

Now only the great fallen timbers sleep under the moss and the berry brush. It is a lonesome place of shadows and mysterious voices in the wind. Each night just as the sun disappears into the sea, the owls return, and their calls echo through the darkness.

The Boy and The Loon

MANY GENERATIONS AGO, THERE LIVED A HANDSOME YOUNG BOY. THE PEOPLE ADMIRED HIM VERY MUCH BECAUSE HE WAS TALL AND STRAIGHT, AND HE HAD A FINE VOICE FOR SINGING.

On sunny days the boy would sit in front of his house combing and oiling his long black hair and painting his face. He was born of a noble family and knew that a great heritage awaited him as leader of his people.

The boy's favorite place was a small lake deep in the forest behind the village. The lake was surrounded by ancient cedar and hemlock trees. It was a quiet, beautiful place where the boy could bathe and then rub his body with hemlock branches. This ritual would purify him so he could sing the songs of power and call upon the spirits for strength and wisdom. One day, as the boy was preparing to bathe in the cool dark waters, there was a slight movement in the grass near the shore. The boy saw it and was curious. He put on his robe, strode over to the spot where he had seen the motion, and parted the dense grass.

A great loon lay there. It was caught by its long slender neck in the noose of a mink trap. The loon was weak and close to death. It stared helplessly at the boy. Its strange red eyes pleaded silently for help.

14

The boy turned to go but suddenly stopped. He thought of the suffering in the eyes of the poor creature. Wheeling around the boy knelt down and took out a mussel shell knife that he wore around his neck on a string. He cut the strong sinews of the noose and freed the loon.

Immediately the loon began to breathe easier. The boy held the bird against his body to give it warmth. After awhile the loon grew stronger and was able to stand. The boy helped the loon to the shore of the lake and into the water, where it swam slowly away.

"Wait," said the boy. "Take this. It will heal you." From around his neck, the boy took a necklace made of the *ikwah* shells so prized by his people for trade and ornament.

The boy tossed the beautiful necklace to the loon. It caught on the loon's long neck and spun 'round and 'round until it looked like the loon was wearing a white collar of shells. The loon paddled silently out into the lake, circled once, then dove deep into the water.

The boy watched and watched for the loon to surface, but it had disappeared. Finally the boy returned to his place by the lake and took off his robe. He jumped into the water and bathed himself thoroughly. Then he climbed out and rubbed himself with hemlock branches until his skin glowed. The boy wanted so much to be a strong leader for his people.

Time passed and, alas, the healthy young boy fell ill. A wasting sickness caused terrible sores to appear on his skin and his hair and teeth to fall out. The people who had loved and respected the boy were frightened and ran away. Even his friends abandoned him.

Most of the day the boy hid in his house, venturing out only in the evening when it was near dark. The boy was weak and ashamed. He knew he would never be able to lead his people now, for even he was repulsed by his sickly image.

The boy could bear it no longer. He said good-bye to his parents and left to end his wretched existence. ✳ He knew the people would be better off without him, and they would soon forget him.

Sick at heart the boy followed the familiar path to the lonely lake. When he got there, he filled his robe with stones and jumped into the water. Down, down he sank into the dark, cold depths. The light faded, and he grew weaker and weaker. Suddenly the boy felt himself being pulled upward. 🐢 Up he rose until he reached the surface and sucked air into his lungs. When the boy looked around, there beside him was a great loon. Around its neck was a necklace of *ikwah* shells. 🜋

"I know you," said the loon in a strange chattering voice. "You were kind to me. You

saved me,
or at least
you thought
you did. You
were generous.
You gave me this
fine necklace and your
good wishes. Now I will
help you." 🐟

"But how can you help
me?" asked the boy. "You are
just a loon!"

"But I am rather more than a loon,"
said the bird. "Indeed, I am the Chief of
all Loons."

Then Loon Chief told the boy how he had often seen him
at the lake bathing and seeking supernatural power.

"I wanted to test you, so I put my head into that mink
trap," confessed Loon Chief. ✖ "Then I waited to see if you
would show me a kindness. You did. Now I will heal you."

🪶 Loon Chief told the boy to climb onto his back. Then
together they flew out over the lake.

"We will cross the lake four times," said Loon Chief.
"Each time you must sing the song that I give you. Then I will

dive into the lake four times. You must hold fast to my neck, because I will go deep to the floor of the lake. There you will see the houses of the Loon People, a secret that has been kept since the beginning of time. I share this secret with you because you are worthy."

Four times Loon Chief sped across the lake. Four times he dove into the deep waters. The boy felt as if his lungs would burst, but he held on fast. Each time they surfaced the young boy saw there were fewer sores on his body and his hair was growing back. On the fourth and last dive, the boy was cleansed of the sickness.

"I have healed you," said Loon Chief. "Now I will make you a great shaman, and you will use my power to do good."

"Do good for whom?" asked the boy.

"For your people," said Loon Chief.

"But they hated me because I was sick and ugly!" cried the boy.

"You must forgive your people. You must forget the sickness and remember only the songs of power I give you. You must help the people even though they ignored you in your suffering."

"This I will do!" said the boy.

For a long time Loon Chief instructed the young man at the lake. Other loons came crowding about, singing and chattering. The boy grew strong and wise. Finally Loon Chief revealed himself to the boy. He took off his robe and mask and appeared as a handsome, glowing human being. He said

to the boy, "You have learned well! I will give you my robe. You must wear it when you counsel and heal the people."

With that Loon Chief draped his robe over the boy's shoulders. "Your life will be long and useful," he said. "In the end I will see you again. Farewell young friend. Return to your people."

The boy hurried down the path. As he ran faster and faster, Loon Chief's robe lifted him. He spread his arms wide and they became wings. ⚡ The boy flew to the village, settling down in front of the great cedar house where his family dwelled. He folded the robe over his arm and walked in.

The people saw him and were frightened. They believed he was a ghost! The boy thought he had been gone four days, but actually he had been away for four long years.

At first the people were wary of the boy, but finally they became used to the idea that he had returned. He began to help people when they were sick or wounded in hunting or fishing accidents. As directed by Loon Chief, he counseled and healed the people. They loved him for all his shaman's wisdom. And when he sang the loon songs, the people knew that all would be well.

The boy-shaman grew old, and his shiny black hair turned white. One day he heard the loons calling. He knew that it was time to visit the lake for the last time. He put on his loon robe and stood before the people of the village. "I must go now," he said. "But I will not be far away. You cannot see me, but you will hear me in the cry of the loons. Go to the lake and bathe. It is a source of power and healing. I will always be there with my guardian loons."

Then the shaman spread his arms and flew into the air. He soared over the tall cedars and hemlocks and vanished into the lake forever!

Thereafter when the people were in trouble they listened for the cries of the loons. They would go to the lake, seek out its healing power, and remember the young boy who was healed by it and who healed them. They too became more tolerant of others in their sicknesses and misfortunes.

RAVEN & SEA GULL

ONE DAY SEA GULL BECAME JEALOUS OF THE DAYLIGHT. HE LONGED TO POSSESS IT AND KEEP IT ALL TO HIMSELF. HE CALLED UPON HIS *DLUGWEE,* HIS SUPERNATURAL TREASURE, TO HELP HIM CAPTURE THE DAYLIGHT.

After Sea Gull had caught the daylight, he rolled it into a ball, carried it into his house, and hid it in a large wooden chest. When he closed the heavy lid the world was plunged into the longest, blackest night that had ever been!

All the animal people blundered about in the darkness. They had to feel their way around, and it was nearly impossible to find food. They suffered and starved.

Finally Raven, who was also wandering about in the darkness, catching his long beak in the bushes and the trees, decided he must do something to help the people. Raven knew what had really happened to the daylight. He gathered the people and spoke to them.

"I know where the daylight has gone," said Raven. "And I am the only one who can bring it back. But you must all hold good thoughts for me as I set about this task."

As Raven groped his way to a nearby beach, he began to form a tricky plan to recapture the daylight from Sea Gull. In the tidal pools Raven carefully searched until he found some small sea urchins. Raven gathered many sea urchins and put them in the basket he had brought along. When the basket was full Raven sucked the tender flesh out of the sea urchins,

saving the sharp spiny shells. Then he felt his way through the darkness to the house of Sea Gull.

Outside the door Raven called out in a loud voice, "Waahhh, it is Raven. Sea Gull, Old *Tligwee,* come out and greet me."

Sea Gull heard Raven's voice, but he was not fond of Raven. Raven always stayed too long and ate too much and sang too loud. But Sea Gull knew he must greet his cousin properly or the people would despise him for being stingy and disrespectful to his kinsman. So Sea Gull shuffled out to greet Raven.

Meanwhile Raven had scattered the sharp sea urchin spines all around the door of Sea Gull's house. As Sea Gull stepped through the doorway one of his big flat feet came down upon a shell.

"Ooow, ooow, ooooow," he cried as his other big foot came down upon more sharp spines.

Sea Gull tumbled back into the house yelling at the top of his voice, "Oh my feet, my feet, my poor, poor feet! Oh they hurt! They hurt! They hurt!"

Stepping over the sea urchin shells Raven quickly slipped into the house. "My dear cousin, whatever is the matter?" asked Raven.

"Oh my feet, my feet, my poor, poor feet!" cried Sea Gull, hopping from foot to foot. "They hurt! They hurt! They hurt!"

"Let me help you," crooned Raven as he reached out and grabbed Sea Gull by his skinny leg. "Even in this darkness I can tell that you have something sticking in your foot."

"Yes, and it hurts. It hurts. It hurts!" whined Sea Gull.

"If I just had a knife I might be able to help you," said Raven smiling to himself.

"Here, take this," cried Sea Gull as he handed Raven a small knife that he always wore around his neck.

Raven quickly turned Sea Gull upside down and began to dig roughly at Sea Gull's foot with the knife. Sea Gull screamed and flapped his wings until the house was filled with his feathers.

"Oh! My feet! My feet! My poor, poor feet!" cried Sea Gull. "They hurt! They hurt! They hurt!"

"If I had a little light I could do a better job," said Raven impatiently.

"Over there, over there!" squawked Sea Gull as he flapped a wing in the direction of the great wooden chest. "Open it! Open the chest, but only a little!"

Raven scurried to the chest and eased the lid up until a crack of daylight shot into the room. He ran back to dig once more at Sea Gull's foot.

Sea Gull screamed again, "My feet! They hurt! They hurt! They hurt!"

"If only I had more light I could work quickly and be done with this," said the sly Raven.

"Open the chest a little more," cried Sea Gull. "But be

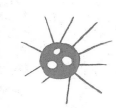

careful. Do not let the daylight out!" ▲▲▲

Raven went to the chest and raised the lid further. The room grew brighter. Back he ran to Sea Gull where he began tugging at the spines in the old bird's foot.

❋ "Ooow!" wailed Sea Gull. "It hurts! It hurts! It hurts!"

"I cannot get them," snapped Raven without sympathy. "It is just not light enough in here to see all of the spines in your foot."

"Open the chest! Open the chest!" squawked Sea Gull, his voice so hoarse from screaming that he could hardly be understood. ❧

With that Raven rushed across the room, threw back the lid of the chest, and watched happily as the daylight spilled out. Once again the world was bright and beautiful! ⸸

The animal people rejoiced! Raven had tricked old Sea Gull and freed the daylight. And what became of Sea Gull? He never quite got over the sea urchin spines in his feet. To this day when you sit on the beach you can see Sea Gull walking as if his feet hurt, and you can hear him crying "Caneee, caneee," as he mourns the loss of his treasured daylight.

POOGWEESE

OUR ANCESTORS BELIEVED THERE WERE REALMS IN THIS WORLD
WHERE SUPERNATURAL BEINGS LIVED. IN THE SKY LIVED A GREAT
CLAN OF THUNDERBIRDS, THE BIRDS OF THE WINTER CEREMONIAL.
IN ANOTHER REALM FAR BENEATH THE EARTH, WHERE EVERY-
THING WAS BACKWARDS, DWELLED THE GHOSTS. BUT THE RICH-
EST REALM OF ALL WAS BENEATH THE SEA. THIS IS THE STORY OF
HOW OUR PEOPLE LEARNED OF THE UNDERSEA WORLD.

The people of the village were fearful. Fishing had been poor for a long time, and their stores of dried fish were almost gone. Winter would soon be upon them, and they might starve. Every day the village fishermen went out to sea and let down their nets. They fished and fished but caught nothing. The sea seemed without life.

One day the fishermen took their canoes off Bird Island. They let their nets sink deeper and deeper into the cold waters. Then they waited. After awhile there was a strong tugging at the lines. The fishermen knew something very large must be in the net.

It took all hands to pull the heavy net up and heave it into the canoe. Tangled in the net was a strange being like nothing the fishermen had ever seen before! It was clothed in seaweed and appeared to be something like a man. It had huge front teeth and long scraggly hair.

The creature lay there making a squeaking noise. Finally it spoke. "You do not know me, so I will tell you. I am Poogweese, the Merman. I am part man and part fish. I dwell in the world beneath the sea. I am chief messenger of

Goomaquay, the lord who controls all the wealth of the ocean. I am his trusted messenger. With the help of the gulls and the loons and the sawbilled ducks, I carry the will of Goomaquay throughout his undersea domain."

The astonished fishermen listened and stared at the strange creature. They did not know what to do. They were afraid if they let Poogweese go he would tell Goomaquay about his captors. This mighty ruler of the sea might get angry and send many great storms. The fishermen would never have any luck fishing again.

"I know what you are thinking," said Poogweese. "You are thinking that if you let me go I will tell Lord Goomaquay. I can understand how you might well be afraid of me, and you certainly should be afraid of my master, but let us strike a bargain."

Then Poogweese explained that if the fishermen would release him to his ocean home he would talk to his master about the fishermen's kindness and about the poor fishing they had endured.

"When Lord Goomaquay realizes that you have freed me and that you know of his existence perhaps life will be better for you," said Poogweese. "And for my thanks I will give you my mask and my song as a gift."

The fishermen looked at one another. They knew they had no choice but to send this powerful creature back to the deep. So they accepted his offer. They could only hope their goodwill would please Lord Goomaquay and that he would improve the fishing and protect them from the great storms.

So the fishermen freed Poogweese from the net. He flopped over the side of the canoe and disappeared into the water. The fishermen looked at one another. One of them said, "He didn't leave us his mask or his song. Maybe he tricked us! Maybe he lied!" Another fisherman cried, "No,

the supernatural ones do not lie." 🦫

Suddenly a shower of bubbles rose from the sea, and the mask of Poogweese floated to the surface. The fishermen pulled the mask from the water and held it. Then they heard a faint sound. It was weak at first, but they listened and listened, and soon the song of Poogweese filled their ears.

The song described the great house made of copper on the floor of the sea just off Bird Island. 🐝 This was the home of Lord Goomaquay and all of his retinue of sea monsters and great creatures from the depths.

The fishermen were pleased. The weather was fair and the tides were right. They cast out their nets and caught many fish. Then the fishermen carefully wrapped the mask and took it home. 🐚 They kept it hidden until the next great potlatch of their people. There they showed the mask proudly and described how it had come to them as a gift from Poogweese and Goomaquay, the Lord of the Undersea.

For all time the people would cherish the mask of Poogweese, for it reminded them of their ancestors' adventure in the beginning of time when men and supernatural spirits talked together. It reminded them why their fishermen were successful and safe upon the sea and why their village was wealthy. Through this fateful encounter with Poogweese, the Merman, the people would feel kin to all the beings within the sea forever. 🪶

BEAVER FACE

ONCE THERE WAS A LARGE VILLAGE ON THE EDGE OF THE DENSE GREEN FOREST. THERE WERE MANY CHILDREN IN THE VILLAGE. THEY OFTEN PLAYED AROUND THE HOUSES AND ALONG THE SHORE. THEY BUILT TOY CANOES. THEY SKIPPED ROCKS ACROSS THE WATER. THEY GATHERED SEASHELLS. BUT THEY NEVER WANDERED INTO THE FOREST, FOR THEY KNEW IT WAS A SCARY PLACE WHERE MYSTERIOUS THINGS HAPPENED AND SUPERNATURAL BEINGS LIVED.

One of the children was a special little girl. When she was born her parents discovered that her upper lip had not grown together properly. It was divided under her nose so that her teeth showed through the cleft. Because she looked different some of the children were cruel to her. They called her Beaver Face.

But Beaver Face was a brave and clever girl. She chose to ignore their taunts. In fact, she was so full of goodwill and laughter that many of the other children respected her as a good friend.

One day the children were playing near the edge of the forest. Suddenly a child pointed into the darkness of the trees and screamed, "Something is there! It is huge with big eyes, and it is watching us!"

The frightened children flew like a flock of birds down the path to the village and to safety. When the parents heard about the awful being in the woods they thought the children were joking. "Do not be afraid. Go back and play. Nothing

will harm you as long as you do not go into the forest,"
they said.

The children returned to their play, but this time
they were not quite so near the trees as before. They were
cautious and watchful for awhile, but then, children being
children, they forgot their fear and drew nearer and nearer
to the forest.

Suddenly a dark figure, twice as tall as a man, crashed out
of the brush. Its body was covered with shaggy black fur. It
had long arms, huge feet, and wild glaring eyes.

The children knew immediately from the stories the
elders had told them that this was Tsonoqua, the Timber
Giant, the devourer of children!

On her back the fearsome Tsonoqua carried a large bur-
den basket. Quickly she began snatching up the children, just
like picking berries from a bush. She rubbed pitch on their
eyes and tossed each of them over her shoulder into the basket. One after another Tsonoqua caught the children. The
last was Beaver Face.

As the frightened children bumped along in the basket
they could see nothing. They could only feel the motion of
the creature as it lumbered with great strides deeper and
deeper into the forest. The children wept with fear. All
except Beaver Face, who kept her wits about her and began to
plan a way out of this difficulty.

In a little workbasket that was always tied to her belt,
Beaver Face found a ball of mountain goat fat. She put it into
her mouth and chewed it until it became very soft. Then she
rubbed the fat on her eyes and easily wiped away the pitch.
She smeared fat on the eyes of the other children, and they
too were able to wipe away the pitch and see again.

Then Beaver Face took out a small mussel shell knife and
began to cut at the bottom of the basket. At last she made a

hole big enough for the children to squeeze through. Beaver Face let the children down through the hole one by one so they could drop quietly to the ground. To each one she whispered, "Run to the village! Tell the warriors to arm themselves and follow the trail of this monster!"

The last child escaped, and only Beaver Face remained in the basket. She had saved the others, but now she was alone with the horrible creature.

Suddenly Tsonoqua stopped and slipped the basket from her back. The creature peered inside and saw that the basket was empty except for one small child.

"Aargh!" cried the enraged Tsonoqua. "Are you the one responsible for losing my dinner? Was it you who ruined my basket?"

"Yes!" said the brave little Beaver Face. "I am the one. You can blame me!"

"And so I will!" said Tsonoqua. "You are not very fat and will not make much of a meal, but I will eat you for a snack anyway."

"Eat me if you must," said Beaver Face. "At least my friends are safely back in the village."

"No one is safe from me! I am the Timber Giant!" roared Tsonoqua in anger.

"That may be," replied Beaver Face, "but you have only me to eat. The others have escaped."

At that moment Tsonoqua noticed the beautiful abalone shell earrings in Beaver Face's ears. They sparkled like the sun on deep seawater. Tsonoqua loved bright, shiny ornaments, so she said, "I want a pair of earrings like yours, then I will be beautiful."

Beaver Face could hardly keep from laughing, for she knew that even the most wonderful earrings would never make this horrible creature look beautiful. Then Beaver Face had an idea.

"If you let me go I will give you my earrings," said the quick-witted Beaver Face.

"Why should I do that?" asked Tsonoqua. "I will have your earrings after I eat you anyway!"

Beaver Face replied quickly. "Yes, you will have my earrings, but without holes in your ears you cannot wear them!"

"That is right," said Tsonoqua. "So before I eat you, you will pierce my ears."

"I will need a sharp stake and a stone maul," said Beaver Face.

"Very well," said Tsonoqua impatiently. "My house is nearby, and I will find the tools you need."

Tsonoqua plucked up little Beaver Face and, in a dozen swift strides, arrived at a great house deep in the forest.

As she went inside Tsonoqua clutched Beaver Face tightly in her big ugly hand. The little girl stared around the gloomy room in amazement. There were riches piled from floor to ceiling. There were shining coppers, mountain goat skins, soft sea otter and ermine pelts, abalone shells, and woolen blankets.

"This should do nicely," said Tsonoqua gruffly as she stooped to pick up a sharp stake and stone maul from the floor.

"Oh yes!" replied Beaver Face eagerly. "I can pierce your ears, and then you can eat me."

"Rest assured that I will eat you!" said Tsonoqua with a glimmer in her eye.

"But first you must put me down," said Beaver Face. "Then you must lie down so I can reach your ears."

Tsonoqua, who was very hungry by now and quite anxious to wear the earrings, quickly stretched out on the dirt floor of the house.

"I must drive this stake through your ear to make a hole," said Beaver Face. "It may hurt a little."

"Nothing hurts me!" bragged Tsonoqua. "I am not afraid of anything. Make the hole!"

The clever Beaver Face drove the stake through the lower part of Tsonoqua's ear and deep into the dirt.

"I need another stake," said Beaver Face.

"Get the one by the firepit. And hurry!" growled Tsonoqua. 🐦

Beaver Face grabbed the second stake and pounded it through Tsonoqua's other earlobe, firmly anchoring the stake in the ground. Now the great Tsonoqua was pinned to the ground by her ears! ➳

Beaver Face scampered to the head of Tsonoqua. With all her might she struck the creature on the forehead with the stone maul. 🜁

The Timber Giant was dead! Just then warriors from the village arrived, followed by all of the mothers and grandmothers and barking dogs. 🐦

"How did this creature get in this position?" asked Beaver Face's father.

"I did it," said Beaver Face proudly. "I drove the stakes into Tsonoqua's ears, pinned her to the ground, and killed her!"

The villagers could not believe such a tiny child could kill the Timber Giant, but there was no one else who could have done it. It had to have been Beaver Face!

The villagers rejoiced. They began to gather the great bundles of valuable blankets and furs to take back to the village. Only the father of Beaver Face refused to take any wealth from the house of Tsonoqua. He held his daughter up for all to see and said, "You are brighter than the sun and wise beyond your years. You saved the children. You killed the monster, and it will never come back!"

"Do not be so sure," said Beaver Face. "Tsonoqua has great power. Perhaps we should go quickly and leave the creature and the house."

But even as Beaver Face spoke the villagers set the house afire. Flames and black clouds of smoke roared into the sky. Soon only ashes remained.

The villagers began to kick at the ashes. As the ashes flew into the air a thundering voice rose from the earth. "Though you burn me I will bite you! Though you burn me I will drink your blood!"

With that the ashes turned into mosquitœs and blackflies and hornets and all the stinging pests that plague human beings to this day.

And what became of Beaver Face? No one ever called her by that name again. She became Bright As The Sun, a high-ranking woman in the village, and she lived a long and happy life.

ACKNOWLEDGMENTS

I would like to thank the elders of many tribes who were so kind to pass their stories to me; Chris Normandin
for the sensitivity she displayed in bringing these stories from the spoken word to the written word;
Steve Beckham for his inspiration and his support of me and so many Native Americans.

CHIEF LELOOSKA
1996

A DK INK BOOK

IN ASSOCIATION WITH
CALLAWAY EDITIONS

FIRST AMERICAN EDITION, 1997
2 4 6 8 10 9 7 5 3 1

PUBLISHED IN THE UNITED STATES BY
DK Ink
An imprint of DK Publishing, Inc.
95 Madison Avenue
New York, New York 10016
VISIT US ON THE WORLD WIDE WEB AT HTTP://WWW.DK.COM

A CATALOG RECORD IS AVAILABLE FROM THE LIBRARY OF CONGRESS.

US ISBN 0-7894-2455-X

UK ISBN 0-7513-7125-4

COLOPHON

This book was produced by Callaway Editions, Inc.

Nicholas Callaway, Editorial Director

Andrea Danese, Editor

Jennifer Wagner, Designer

True Sims, Production Director

Paula Litzky, Marketing and Sales Director

All text for this book is set in Mrs Eaves, designed by Zuzana Licko.
All titles, cover, and introductory paragraphs are set in Mantinia, designed by Matthew Carter.

The map on pages 6-7, a wood engraving, was illustrated by John Lawrence.

The CD was produced at Big Music, Inc.
Digital editing and post production by Bruce Buchanan and Michael Lau.

The artwork that appears in this book was photographed by Bill Bachhuber.

This book was printed and bound by Palace Press International under the
supervision of Erik Ko and Ruby Sia.

Printed in China

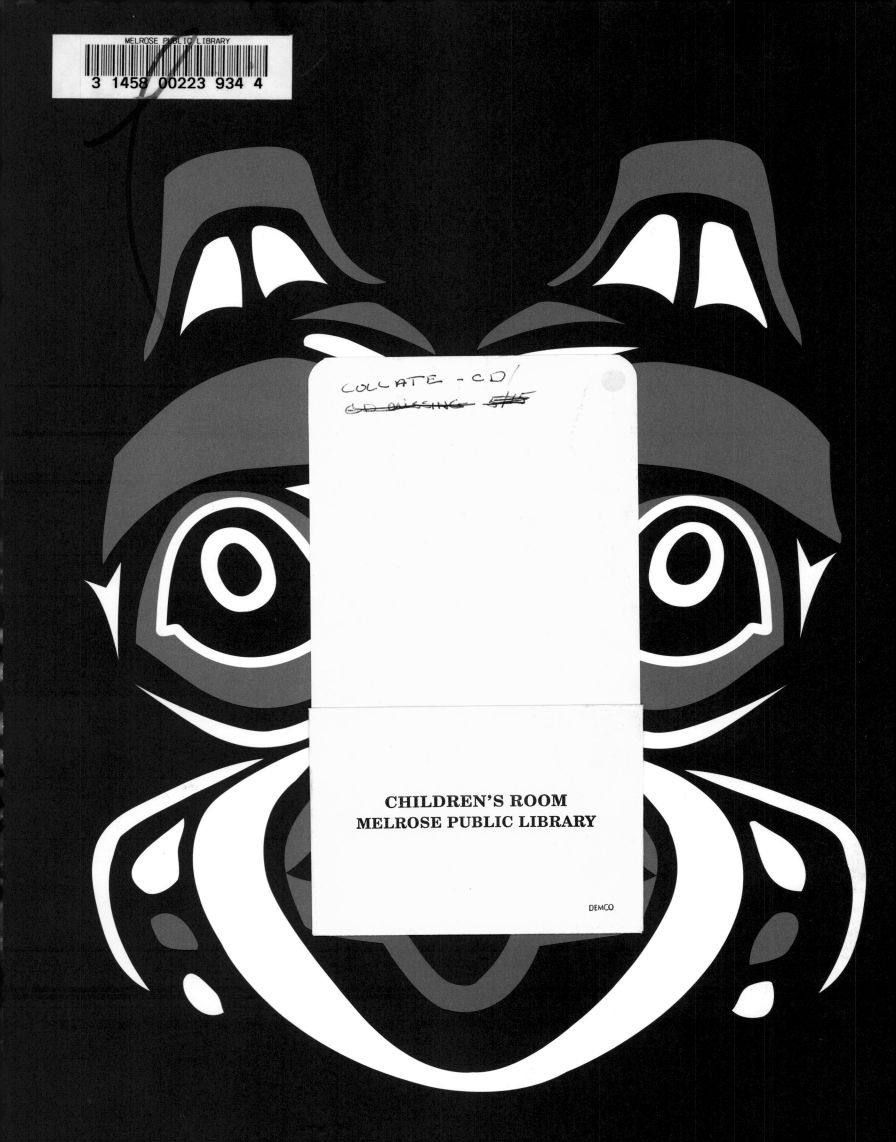